Jr.

200

Discard

Burma Boy

Whittlesey House

McGRAW-HILL BOOK COMPANY, INC.

NEW YORK   TORONTO   LONDON

Burma Boy

by Willis Lindquist
Pictures by
Nicolas Mordvinoff

BURMA BOY

Library of Congress Catalog Card Number: 53–8017

PUBLISHED BY *Whittlesey House*
A division of the McGraw-Hill Book Company, Inc.
PRINTED IN THE UNITED STATES OF AMERICA

Seventh Printing

6

To Chris

This is the way to say the
Burmese words used in this book

Cardamons (CAR-da-mons) large plants
Chinwa (Chin-WA) Haji's home village
Irrawaddy (Ir-ra-WAD-dee) a river in Burma
Kaing grass (KYEng) tall grass
Karen peddler (KA-ren) a peddler from the Karen states
Mango (MANG-go) a tropical fruit
Maung (MONG) Mister
Nullah (NUL-ah) a gully
Oozie (OO-zee) an elephant rider
Paddy (PAD-dee) rice
Paijaik (PIE-jike) a boy helper
Pye-dog (Pie dog) a stray dog
Sambur deer (SAM-ber) a deer of Asia
Sayah (SIGH-ah) witch doctor
Tamarind (TAM-a-rind) a tropical tree
Thakin (THAK-in) Master
Yomaks (YO-maks) mountain range of Burma

Contents

1

Runaway Elephant

Stars twinkled over the teak forest of the upper Irrawaddy. The hour was late, but no one could sleep in the elephant camp, least of all the boy Haji. Word had come down from the jungle country to the north that mighty Majda Koom, the father of all elephants, had been seen in the hills with a herd of wild elephants.

For two long years Haji had awaited news of the elephant he loved so dearly, and now he was almost afraid to believe what he heard. Joy bubbled up in him.

"Majda Koom has been seen! He is alive!" his heart sang over and over again. "He lives! He did not fall into an elephant trap. The hunters were not able to harm him. Some day he will come back to me and we will be together again in the jungle."

Haji edged closer to where the oozies, as the brown-skinned Burman elephant riders were called, sat about their campfires. They spoke of Majda Koom in hushed voices. Many of them had known the great elephant well before he ran away and became a wild beast in the jungle. Even those who were new in camp had heard of him, for the fame of Majda Koom had spread to the far corners of Burma, from the jade-green jungles of Shan to the distant borders of Tibet and India.

"Never was there an elephant like him," said an oozie. "His tusks are as thick around as the pillars in the pagoda temple at Chinwa."

"For thirty years," declared a wrinkled oozie, "Majda Koom did the work of three elephants in this very teak forest. He stood over other elephants as a mountain stands over the hills. Yet, truly, he was gentle as a fawn till the madness came over him."

"It was even so," whispered Haji to his young friend Byoo.

Though only thirteen years of age, Haji could have

told them much about the mighty elephant his father had ridden and cared for so long. But he said nothing. It was not polite for a boy to speak before his elders.

"Why did Majda Koom run away?" asked a new oozie.

The wrinkled one poked into the campfire with a stick. Sparks swirled up into the purple night and disappeared in the arching branches of the fig trees. "Some say it was grief that drove him into the jungle. Who can say what is in the mind of an elephant who has lost his master?"

No one tried to answer that, though several oozies glanced at Haji, as if they thought he might know.

The man who had brought the news from the north spoke up: "They say Madja Koom has killed all who tried to capture him. Now he leads a herd of wild elephants. Only a week ago they trampled a village and drove off the people. Many might have been killed had they not been quick. I think there will be much trouble with the big bull."

Byoo tugged at Haji's arm. "The boys," he whispered. "They are calling you."

Haji looked at the campfire where his young friends were gathered. They were looking at him and making signs that he should come. Like himself, they were all ground helpers. They handled the big elephant chains, hooked them around the teak logs that were to be dragged to the river, and took their orders from the oozies who rode the elephants.

Haji went to join them. With them he could speak freely. They felt as he did about elephants. They loved elephants, and each lived only for the day when he would be given an elephant to ride and command.

But there were never enough elephants to go around. Some of the boys would have to be content as camp cooks, others as tree choppers. Some would be chosen to ride the teak logs down the river to the sawmill. Only a few lucky ones who showed special skill with the elephants would ever have a chance to become oozies.

"Haji," said one of the boys, "would you be afraid to go out and look for Majda Koom?"

Byoo laughed. "Why should he be afraid? He was climbing on Majda Koom's tusks almost before he could walk. Some say Majda brushed the flies away from Haji while he slept."

They all laughed.

"Wah!" Haji said, grinning. "That is not true about the flies." He liked the way they were looking at him, with wide eyes, as if they expected some wonderful thing of him now that the mightiest of all elephants had been seen. "But I do remember this: If a wild animal ever came too close to me, Majda Koom was sure to chase it away."

"He even chased me away once when I was fighting with Haji," laughed Byoo. "Majda Koom was very

13

jealous. He never liked it when I played with Haji. If I did not go away soon enough to suit him, he would pick Haji up and carry him off into the jungle."

"It was even so," Haji agreed. "When I was older, I went always into the jungle to be with Majda Koom on his resting days. I would ride on his head and watch the tiger and the water buffalo run away when we came close. With Majda to protect me, I felt like the prince of all the jungle. There was nothing to fear."

"All that was long ago," said one of the boys. "Majda Koom is wild now. They say he hates all men. I would not trust him."

A smile came to Haji's lips. They did not know how much Majda Koom loved him. "I would never be afraid to trust him," he said. "Majda would know me."

"Look!" Byoo whispered. "Oo Yan comes. There is bad news for someone this night."

The low murmur of voices died quickly away as Oo Yan, the chief of the oozies, walked from fire to fire. He was clearly searching for someone. All eyes turned to follow him anxiously. He did not walk among them often at night and they were more than curious about his business.

He stopped before Haji. "You!" he said, pointing. "Come with me. Thakin Jensen would speak with you."

Haji's heart took a sudden dive. He swallowed. "With—with me?" He was certain a mistake had been made. The white master, Thakin Jensen, was a person of great importance. He was boss man for the Rangoon Lumber Company, which owned all the elephants. He did not even know Haji by name. What could he want of him?

2

Oo Yan's Plan

"Come," said Oo Yan again, more firmly this time, and turned back the way he had come.

Haji rose and followed on stiff legs. All were watching him now, and his heart began racing with fear. There were few who could please the stern thakin.

"Have I done some wrong?" Haji asked anxiously. "Please, Maung Oo Yan, tell him not to send me away from the elephant camp."

Oo Yan did not bother to answer him. They entered the jungle darkness. Fireflies twinkled about them. A jackal howled in the lonely hills, and from all sides came the ringing of wooden elephant bells.

No two elephant bells ever sounded alike, for each oozie made the bell for his own elephant. He carved

it out of a chunk of teakwood, and fixed two clappers to it, one on each side, hanging outside the bell.

Oo Yan and Haji reached the lighted tent and, as they entered, Thakin Jensen looked up from his papers and stared at Haji. He seemed surprised and not at all pleased.

"Have you lost your mind?" he asked Oo Yan angrily. "This is only a child."

"He is the one, thakin. He is Haji, the son of the oozie who trained and worked Majda Koom for thirty years." Oo Yan placed a hand on Haji's shoulder. "Haji was born in the elephant camp. Most of his days were spent in the shadow of the big elephant. He played at its feet. With my own eyes I have seen him use the elephant's trunk for a swing. They went off into the jungle, the two of them, and swam in the river together."

Haji heard the words and felt proud. He stood as straight and tall as he could.

"And now you expect miracles of this boy?" asked Thakin Jensen.

Oo Yan was not disturbed. "Majda Koom loved only two—his oozie and this boy. When his oozie was injured by the falling tree, we sent the family and the boy back to live in the rice village of Chinwa. That was when the elephant went wild, was it not?"

"What are you trying to say?"

"Why did the elephant come into our camp night after night?" asked Oo Yan. "There is only one explanation. He came to search for the boy and the oozie and could not find them. His grief was such that none could go near him."

"That was your opinion," said Thakin Jensen. "We brought the boy back here. What good has it done?"

"We brought him back too late. Majda Koom had already disappeared in the jungle."

Thakin Jensen lighted his pipe and shook his head. "It's no good, Oo Yan. It's been all of two years since the beast went wild. My best oozies were unable to capture him. He killed the last two who tried. He's gone mad, I tell you. He's a killer."

Haji trembled with sudden rage. He wanted to shout that it was not so. Majda Koom was not mad. It was all he could do to hold in the words by pressing his lips tightly together.

"Love is a power above all others," Oo Yan said

gently. "Majda Koom and the wild elephants with him have already destroyed one village. They may destroy others. Many lives may be lost unless Majda Koom is captured, thakin. This boy is our only chance."

So excited was Haji he forgot his fear of Thakin Jensen. "Please, thakin, let me search for him. I am not afraid."

"No!" snapped Thakin Jensen. "I have heard quite enough. Now get out of here, both of you. I will not send a child to face a killer elephant."

They went quickly.

Haji tightened his hands into hard fists as they walked away in the darkness. "I could do it," he said between his teeth. "I could bring Majda Koom back. I know I could! Maybe, if I run away from the elephant camp—"

"If you do, then Thakin Jensen will never allow you to work here again," said Oo Yan. "There is a better way. We shall prove to him that you can handle elephants. Tomorrow I want you to work the young elephant See Po."

Haji looked up in surprise. He was only a paijaik,

as boy helpers were called, and was not expected to know about handling elephants.

"Is it true?" he asked breathlessly. "Am I really to be the oozie of See Po tomorrow?"

"I have said it," replied the chief of the oozies. "It is true you are young, but I have not forgotten how your father trained you to work the big elephant. You did very well. Tomorrow you shall work See Po. If all goes well Thakin Jensen will see your skill and send you to capture Majda Koom."

"I shall try to be a good oozie," Haji promised, so thrilled he could hardly keep from jumping up and down for joy. See Po was small and young, with no tusks, but she was an elephant for all that.

Much as he wanted to tell his young friends, he kept his lips tightly sealed. The plan was a secret that had to be kept between Oo Yan and himself. If Thakin Jensen heard of it, he might spoil everything.

3

Jungle Dawn

He slept very little that night. Sometimes he listened to see if he could hear See Po's wooden bell. Any good oozie could name an elephant a mile away in the jungle merely by listening to the sound of its bell.

No elephant bell Haji had ever heard had the deep rich tones of the one Majda Koom had worn at his neck. Majda had loved his bell, though sometimes when he did not wish to work he would pack mud into the bell, so that Haji and his father would be a long time in finding him. Haji chuckled, remembering how Majda had fooled them.

When at last he fell asleep, he dreamed of bringing back Majda Koom. With Majda Koom as his elephant he would become a great oozie, as his father had been before him.

Before the break of day he was up. With a white cloth wrapped about his hips and another about his head in a loose turban, he went to the elephant watering place by the river.

There, hobbled with chains on their front legs, the working elephants had been given their freedom to wander in the jungle and to feed during the night.

The tracks of elephants were everywhere in the soft mud. Some were several days old. Haji looked only for fresh tracks. There were many of these, but the daintiest of all were those of See Po. Her front pads were as round as cooking pots, her hind ones narrower, shaped rather like coconuts.

He followed her tracks with the skill of an experienced oozie, for many were the times he had trailed Majda Koom with his father in the half-light of morning.

See Po's tracks led through the marsh grasses where the snipe and the wild geese had their nests. There were many frogs, and they leaped out of his path as he came. He caught one of them because he had

many wonderful things to tell. He had always liked
talking to frogs. They blinked so wisely as he talked
that he was certain they understood everything.

Up over a hill of jack trees went the trail. Now
and then See Po had paused to eat branches and

leaves from the trees, or tufts of short grass. Every
bamboo clump in her path had been torn apart and
stripped of its tender green shoots.

A brown and yellow weaver bird scolded Haji from
the fronds of a tamarind tree. He grinned up at her.
"Have no fear, little friend. It is only Haji, seeking
his elephant."

24

He could hardly blame the weaver bird for being upset. It probably had not slept very well. Right under its tree was a flat place in the grass where See Po had made her bed. And See Po snored!

With his heart singing the song of morning, Haji went on. He met a sambur deer and a grandfather porcupine on the trail and shouted cheery greetings. He wanted all the creatures in the jungle to be happy on this very special morning, for today he was an oozie.

But then, quite unexpectedly, he came upon the tracks of a large tiger. Jungle cats were not interested in elephants as a rule. Yet the tracks of this one crossed and recrossed See Po's trail.

Haji was puzzled at first. He dropped to his hands and knees and examined the tiger's tracks more closely. He found dark, wet drops of blood. Tiger's blood! Somehow, the big cat had been wounded, and a wounded cat would attack anything in the jungle, even an elephant.

For another mile the tiger had followed See Po's trail. Finally, it had lost interest and gone about other business. Haji felt better.

On a ridge he paused to listen for the sound of the wooden bell that hung from See Po's neck. All he heard was the faint moo-aw, moo-aw of a wild water buffalo from some distant wallow.

See Po's trail led uphill again, toward the bamboo clumps above. But Haji did not follow. From his experience with elephants, he knew See Po would soon have her fill of bamboo. Then she would head down again to feed on the sweet kaing grass that grew in the nullah, the gully at the foot of the slope.

He started down the slope toward the nullah. There he would find her now, he felt certain. The slope grew steep and rocky. He had to pick his way carefully through thorny brush. Everything about him was strange and new. He wondered why he and his father had never come this way.

Ahead, large boulders suddenly loomed against the sky of gray morning like weird monsters. It was then, with a catch in his breath, that he recognized the evil place. At campfires he had heard that bats sometimes flew up from the boulders in dark clouds. The wicked nats—the bad spirits of the jungle—were said to meet there in the dark of the moon and take the shape of bats.

With a little shiver up his spine, Haji turned and went wide of the place. It was a very unlucky chance that had brought him this way. Wise oozies always carried charms to protect themselves against evil nats. But Haji had no charm.

In his haste to get away, he stumbled on a stone. He wondered fearfully if the nats had cursed him for coming so close. If they had it would mean bad luck for him. With all his heart he wished he could see a cobra slither across his path. Then all would be well. The sight of a cobra, as everyone in the Burma jungle knows, brings good luck.

Several times Haji paused to listen for See Po's bell. What was the matter, he wondered. Why couldn't he hear it? Had the evil nats stopped the bell from singing?

He began to run like a frightened deer. "If I do not find See Po," he told himself, "Thakin Jensen will be very angry. He will have me thrown out of the elephant camp."

Then he would never live with the elephants again.

He would have no chance to go in search of Majda Koom. It was too terrible a fate to think about.

On and on he ran till he reached the tall sea of kaing grass in the nullah. Even then he could not hear the sound of See Po's bell. But once more he came across the tracks of a jungle cat and saw where the creature had entered the tall grass. Along its trail were drops of blood, shiny and fresh.

"Wah!" he exclaimed. "The very same wounded tiger that followed See Po!"

He hurried on, keeping a wide space between himself and the tall grass. Perhaps he had gone half a mile from the tracks of the tiger when he heard the sweetest music that ever an oozie knew—the faint ticky-tok, ticky-tok-tok-tok of See Po's wooden bell in the distance.

The voice of the bell grew louder as he approached. "I come! I come!" sang Haji at the top of his voice. See Po had to be warned of his coming so she would not be startled and run away.

His voice echoed so loudly in the lonely hills that it frightened him a little. He glanced back over his shoulder anxiously, hoping the wounded tiger had not heard him, too.

28

4

Charge of the Wounded Tiger

Presently, he could hear the flopping of elephant ears, and the tearing and crunching and blowing that are the sounds of a feeding elephant. He kept singing loudly to calm her fears.

"The eyelids of morning have opened," he sang. "Darkness has folded her wings and there is nothing to fear. Your new oozie seeks for you. It is I, Haji. I come. I come."

The morning song of the oozie went on and on, so that See Po would know exactly where he was at all times. There were no special words he had to use. Any would do. He sang of the flycatcher birds who were sweeping the gray skies above with their long tails. He sang of the eye of day—the sun—which would soon come leaping up from the eastern hills like a great ball of fire.

> *"All is well, little sister!*
> *There is nothing to fear.*
> *My song is for you;*
> *I hope you can hear."*

He came as close as he could to where See Po was feeding without entering the kaing grass. There no oozie would enter. In the thick grass, so tall that it could hide the largest elephant, lurked unseen dangers. There, royal tigers and panthers lay in hiding. There, wild buffalo and the ill-tempered rhinoceros charged and killed without warning.

"Lah! Lah! Lah! Come on! Come on! Come on!" he cried.

The tearing and blowing sounds of See Po's feeding still continued. Every two or three minutes he called again. He chased a lizard from a flat rock and sat down to wait.

There was no use being impatient. Only See Po could know how much food she needed, and she would keep on eating until she was satisfied. Even the best of oozies could not hurry an elephant. When See Po had finished her breakfast and was ready for work, she would come.

He had waited for perhaps ten minutes when suddenly, out of the corner of his eye, he saw a movement in the tall grass. He stiffened. Something was in there, to the left of the feeding elephant.

Changing his tone he called sharply, "Digo lah! Digo lah! Come here! Come here!"

See Po, of course, paid no attention. For several minutes, Haji watched the place where the grass had moved, but he saw nothing more to arouse suspicion.

Finally, See Po stopped eating. All grew quiet in the kaing grass. Even the flopping of elephant ears had ceased, and that meant See Po was listening for his call. This was her way of asking, "Where are you?"

Haji leaped to his feet. "Over here, little sister! Come on!"

He could hear her coming. The grass tops swayed and swirled about her as she pressed through. But even before she came into sight another movement to the left caught Haji's attention.

He sucked in his breath. The thing was moving toward his elephant in quick starts and stops, in the stealthy manner of a jungle cat stalking its victim. Had there been the slightest breeze, See Po might have been able to catch the tiger's scent and rush off to safety, trumpeting her alarm.

But the still morning air hung like a curtain. She had no warning. She came slowly out of the grass, as if she had all the time in the world. She stopped only a few yards in front of Haji, fanning her big ears, raising her trunk high and weaving it from side to side to catch his scent.

Though she was looking right at him, Haji did not dare move so long as her trunk remained in the air. He knew that elephants relied chiefly on their keen sense of smell. Until See Po caught his scent and recognized it, she would not allow him to approach. But finally her trunk came down and she stood there as if to say, "Well, come on. I recognize you now."

"Wah!" said Haji, trying to keep fear out of his voice. "Would you keep stuffing yourself all day? Do you think I have nothing to do but wait for you?"

He had to keep talking, as oozies usually did, so that

33

See Po would sense nothing unusual. "Already the sun shines on the peaks of the Yomaks and, because of you, I have not yet had one bite of breakfast."

Then his voice rang out in firm command. "Hmit! Lie down!"

See Po dropped obediently to her haunches and rolled over on her side. Haji advanced slowly, his eyes round as coins as he watched the grass beyond her for some sign of the tiger.

He saw nothing. But his heart was hammering loudly and his skin prickled as he came up and gave See Po an affectionate pat on her trunk.

"Tah! Get up!" he ordered.

See Po got to her feet. Quickly, he stooped and unfastened the chain from her front legs and tossed it over her withers.

Once more he ordered her down and climbed onto her neck. "Home, little sister! Home!"

It seemed to him that it took her forever to get to her feet. She was just rising when he heard the thrashing of grass behind them. He whirled—and suddenly his heart stood still.

Just a stone's throw away, the big jungle cat streaked out of the tall grass. It snarled as it came in mighty bounds. He saw the open jaws, the flashing fangs. Straight at them it came, and all Haji could do was watch in helpless horror.

See Po trumpeted her alarm. She wheeled to meet the charge, but her great weight made her much too slow.

With a savage leap the tiger was upon her, ripping with its claws, slashing her back with yellow fangs.

The elephant screamed in pain and terror. She reared. Up on her hind legs she went, up and up.

Haji was tossed high, sailing and turning in the air. For an instant he hung between sky and earth. Then he came down with a crash in the tall kaing grass.

That was all he remembered, for suddenly it was very dark and very still.

5

Haji Meets the Great Elephant

Haji blinked and looked up at the kaing grass waving above him, wondering where he was. Then he remembered. The wounded tiger—it had leaped on his elephant's back!

He sat up with a jerk and looked wildly about. Where was the tiger? What had happened to See Po?

He listened, heard nothing but the whispering of morning breezes through the tall grass.

Quickly, he got to his feet. He was stiff and his back hurt a little, but there was no time to worry about himself. He could smell death even before he burst from the kaing grass. See Po was nowhere in sight.

He approached a dark stain on the slope of the nullah. For a long moment, he stared at it. His whole body trembled with weakness, and he wanted to cry and laugh at the same time.

The tiger was dead.

With the keen senses of one born in the jungle, he read the story of the struggle. See Po had reared up and fallen over on her back to crush the tiger beneath her. Then she had trampled it into the earth with her mighty pads and broken every bone in its body. The stained skin was all that remained, and that was as flat as the tiger-skin rug in the thakin's tent.

"Wah!" Haji exclaimed. He was very proud of See Po.

But then he remembered her deep wounds. She was in pain. He had to find her quickly and take her back to Thakin Jensen for treatment.

Her trail led into the tall kaing grass. He followed, though he knew the dangers that lurked there. The trail was long. Hour after hour, he ran at a steady jog trot that ate up the miles. The sun rose over his head and the day grew hot. Perspiration rolled down

his slender brown body. His breath came in torn gasps. But never once did he slacken his pace.

He could tell, from the distance between See Po's tracks, that she was traveling faster than a man could run. That was proof that she was still frightened and in pain. She had never paused for an instant to feed on the kaing grass.

Finally, her trail led into the hills, into the green twilight of jungle shade. Haji was thankful. He drew the cool air into his burning lungs. Even the thorns of the jungle brush that ripped at his arms and legs were easier to bear than the terrible heat of the midday sun.

In a strange part of the jungle he had never seen

before, he came to a brook of clear mountain water. He dropped to the cool mossy bank and drank deeply. He could not resist the temptation to roll into the stream and let the cool water flow over his burning body. How good it felt.

He meant to stay there only for an instant. But he lingered. Something far down the stream, where it widened into a sun-bright pool, suddenly drew his attention. Slowly, as if in a daze, he sat up. It couldn't be true. He rubbed his eyes and looked again.

There was no mistake about it, and it was not a dream! Drinking at the edge of the sunny pool stood the mightiest of all the Burma elephants—his beloved Majda Koom!

What a beauty the big elephant was! His great, curving tusks were more than twice the length of Haji's body, and as thick around as his chest.

In the two long years Majda Koom had lived in the jungle as a wild elephant, he had not changed at all, except that his tusks were darker. Haji's father had spent many hours scrubbing and polishing and keeping them bright. He had been very proud of those tusks, and rightly so, for not in all Burma was there another set of tusks half so magnificent.

Haji remembered, as he stared at the mighty beast, that people said Majda Koom had gone mad, that he was a killer. But these things Haji could not believe. What was there to fear from an old and trusted friend?

Yet, even an old friend should never be taken by surprise in the jungle. Haji rose quietly. Far from being afraid, he was happier than he had been for a long time. He had found Majda Koom. Now, all he had to do was to bring him back into camp.

Step by step, he advanced along the mossy margin of the brook until he was only a stone's throw from the giant elephant.

Then he stopped and called softly: "Majda. Majda Koom."

Up jerked the mighty head. Ears cocked forward like enormous fans.

"I am Haji, the son of your oozie. I have come for you. Lah! Lah! Lah! Don't you remember me, big brother?"

For an instant Majda Koom stared at him. Haji held his breath. The babbling of the brook seemed like a roaring sound in the jungle stillness.

Suddenly the great beast came to life. He smacked the surface of the pool sharply with his trunk—a warning signal of danger—and, turning, disappeared in the jungle as quickly and quietly as a jungle cat.

"Majda Koom!" shouted Haji in sudden alarm. "Come back! Come back! There is no danger. It is Haji who comes for you."

Again and again he called—but in vain. Majda was gone. And from high up on a distant jungle slope came crashing sounds and the trumpeting of a wild elephant herd, put to sudden flight by the warning signal of their leader.

Stunned, Haji stood there staring at the place where Majda had disappeared. His elephant, his beloved Majda Koom, had not recognized him.

He swallowed hard. Tears stung his eyes. He wanted to cry, but the terrible empty feeling within him made him too weak even for that. All his dreams of capturing Majda Koom, all his hopes of becoming the oozie of the great elephant died in his heart. There was nothing left for him.

As if walking in a dream that could not be real, he went back to the trail of See Po. For several hours he followed it without once hearing the sound of See Po's bell.

Finally, when the sun stood low in the western sky, he gave up. Without chain hobbles to hinder her, See Po had traveled so fast and so far that now she could only be caught by oozies mounted on elephants.

It was long after dark when he returned, weary and hungry, to the elephant camp. His young friends and the oozies quickly gathered around him at a campfire. Oo Yan heard their shouts and came running.

"Where have you been?" he demanded angrily. "What did you do with See Po? Where is she?"

Haltingly, Haji told what had happened.

"He lies!" cried an oozie. "Only a toad could be that stupid."

Another said, "Who ever heard of an oozie calling to his elephant when a wounded tiger is near?"

Even Oo Yan looked at him in dismay. "You have lived your years in the jungle," he said. "You know the ways of a wounded tiger. Did you not know it would come when you called to See Po?"

"I—I thought the tiger was far away," Haji mumbled, knowing what a poor excuse it was. He realized now, when it was too late, that he should have waited quietly on the slope of the nullah, waited till the sun grew hot when See Po would come out of the tall grass to seek the cool shade of the jungle.

"The good oozie thinks first of his elephant," Oo Yan said sternly. "Because you did not, your elephant has been injured. We may never find her again. One who thinks so little of elephants belongs in the rice fields of Chinwa."

"Ay, back to the paddy with him," grumbled an oozie. "Is it not the price any of us would have to pay for letting harm come to an elephant? Away with him!"

46

"Even the son of an owl," said another, "should know that once an elephant has been betrayed he becomes difficult to handle."

Haji looked about at the unfriendly faces. The oozies loved their animals. He, by exposing his elephant to danger, had done the one thing none of them could forgive. Now they wanted him banished, sent back to the rice fields of his father's village.

His eyes filled with tears. Never to live with the elephants again—it would be worse than death.

He fell to his knees before the chief oozie. "Mercy, Maung Oo Yan," he sobbed. "Mercy! Kick me! Beat me with staves of split bamboo. Tie me to the tree of the biting ants for an hour. Punish me as you will, but do not send me away."

In the flickering light of the fire Oo Yan's grim face did not soften. "In the morning you go," he said. "Be gone before the sun touches the cardamons."

Haji hung his head and turned to go. He could hear the oozies as they spat in the dust to show their contempt. He stumbled into the darkness, not caring whether he lived or died. It was the end of all things for him.

47

6

Banished

Before any of the others were up the next morning, Haji was well on his way to the valley of rice fields. Even so, it was a full day of walking through jungled foothills and along the dusty yellow road of the bullock carts before he finally came to the village of Chinwa.

He went directly to the house of his father. Like all the other houses of the village, it was made of thatch and bamboo, and stood on high stilts, so that the animals of the jungle could not enter.

There, as the last dusty tatters of the setting sun filtered through the bamboo slats, Haji told of his banishment from the elephant camp.

His crippled father, who had been helpless since

the tree fell on him two years ago, stirred on his straw-mat bed. "The thing is done," he sighed. "My heart is heavy for you, my son."

Haji looked at his mother. Her joyous smile of welcome had faded. Quickly, she came to sit by him and held his hand, sharing his sorrow. His small sister, with her glossy black hair and a jasmin flower above her ear, stared at him. She had been so proud of him. What could she think now?

Haji hung his head. His lips trembled. "If I have offended . . . if . . . if I have brought shame upon this house, my father, then . . . then send me away to some far village."

"Foolish talk," scolded his father gently. "Oo Yan is not without blame in this. He made you an oozie before your time."

The gong in the pagoda temple at the edge of the village sounded the hour of sunset. Haji's mother and sister went down the ladder to prepare the evening meal on the fire before the house. His father spoke of many things to take his mind away from the elephants.

All had been well in the village, he said. But an

49

owl had hooted over the house of the tinker three
nights in a row—a sign of sickness and death. Something very bad would surely have happened had the
tinker not gone to the sayah—the witch doctor—who
made a charm to break the evil spell. The charm
must have been very strong, for there had been no
sickness or death in the tinker's family, and no one
had heard the hoot of an owl since that day.

"With such a powerful charm," said Haji, "I could
have saved See Po from the tiger."

"Nothing is sure," said his father. "I wore the sayah's charm the very day the tree fell on me." His withered hand reached out and touched the wooden bell of Majda Koom, which had been torn from the elephant's neck by the falling tree. "It was Majda Koom who saved my life by lifting the tree from my body."

Haji told of meeting Majda Koom in the jungle. "But he is as wild as any elephant," he said. "He did not know me."

"An elephant's eyes are not sharp at a distance," reminded his father. "And you have changed. You have grown much these past two years."

"But I called to him!"

"Your voice also has changed, my son. It is deeper now. You are no longer the child Majda Koom remembers and loves so well."

Haji could see how hopeless it was. He had changed so much Majda Koom would never again be able to recognize him.

His new life in the village began before dawn the following morning. With his sister leading the way, he went to the pagoda temple and joined the children of Chinwa under the sacred bo tree. They chanted prayers until the gray light of dawn swept the stars from the sky. Then a priest in yellow robes gave out books, long, narrow books made of palm fronds, and the reading lesson began.

Everyone read aloud. Some read slowly, others with great speed. It did not matter, for the books were not all the same anyway.

The priest went to this one and that one, cocking his head, listening for mistakes. Haji, like most of the others, read at the top of his voice, so the priest would think he could read very well and pass him by quickly.

The shrill voices made such a din the monkeys in the bo tree above began jabbering complaints and shaking the branches. Parrots screeched. A pye-dog howled, for the noise hurt its ears, and all the other pye-dogs in the village joined in the swelling chorus.

It was dawn, and no mistake, and the sounds of newborn day thundered over the village of Chinwa.

The reading lesson did not last very long. Before the morning mists had lifted from the lowlands by the river, Haji was in the rice fields with the villagers, busy with the new harvest.

He could not understand why people joked and laughed and sang while they worked so hard in the fields. But then, none of them had ever known how fine it was to live in an elephant camp.

Sometimes he slept by day and sat the night through on one of the bamboo watchtowers that stood over the paddy fields. The precious rice crop had to be guarded carefully now from the animals of the jungle —the sambur deer and wild pigs and buffalo—whose feasting and trampling could do great damage in a single night.

It was rarely lonely on those night watches, Haji discovered. The boys in the towers kept up a constant chatter among themselves to frighten off animals and to keep each other awake. They never tired of asking Haji about the elephants.

"Tell us more about Majda Koom," Ket Kay shouted one night. "Did you ever tease him?"

"Ay. Almost every day when work was done Majda came searching for me," said Haji. "I never found a hiding place where he couldn't smell me out. He liked hunting for me. But best of all he liked to take me to the river and play the water game."

54

"Could he swim?" asked Ket Kay.

"All elephants can swim! You perhaps never saw one swimming because they like better to walk on the deep river bottom and hold up their trunks for air."

"Ay!" laughed the boys in the nearby towers. "That we have seen."

Ket Kay asked, "How did you play the water game?"

Now it was Haji who laughed. "When we came to the deep place in the river I would try to drag his trunk under water so he could not breathe. It was a game to see who could fight the longest under water without breathing. Sometimes I would win and Majda had to throw me off and poke up his trunk for air."

Such happy memories of the big elephant lived always in Haji's mind. Whenever he picked a mango from a tree he was reminded of the times Majda Koom lifted him high, so he could pick the ripest fruit from the tree.

Whenever his father rang the bell of Majda Koom, Haji could almost see the big elephant standing before him.

The clatter and squeaking of a bullock cart made his heart race, for bullock drivers sometimes had news from the elephant camp. One day they brought word that See Po had been caught and was almost well again.

But late one afternoon another sound broke over the peaceful valley of rice fields like a clap of thunder.

7

A Warning From the North

Gongs boomed. Shouts of alarm came from the village. For a stunned moment those in the rice fields stopped to listen. And then they were running, Haji along with them.

"It must be a fire," someone cried.

Ket Kay caught up with Haji at the edge of the village. "Maybe a big storm is coming," he gasped. "See, the people are coming from the houses."

Never had Haji beheld such confusion. People were everywhere in the streets, milling, shouting questions, glancing anxiously toward the sky. No one seemed to know why the alarm had been sounded.

Whole families of monkeys were leaping wildly from one thatch roof to another, headed for safety

among the trees. Pye-dogs barked and scurried for cover.

"To the gong-beating place," yelled Ket Kay in Haji's ear. "Follow me."

Under the houses he ran, with Haji at his heels. They reached the thronged market square just as a Shan pony reared and slashed the air with its hoofs. It broke from its master and went plunging through the crowd, spreading panic and knocking over the fruit stalls of the seller women.

The thundering of the gong ceased suddenly and the beater of the gong held up his hands for silence. People moved toward the wooden platform where he stood.

Above the clamor and bustle came his voice. "Majda Koom!" he cried. "He comes to destroy us. He has gone mad." He beckoned with his hands. "Draw near, you people of Chinwa, while the elders decide how best to protect your lives and your homes."

Haji's blood went cold. Frantically, he pressed through the throng, squeezing and pushing, until he made his way to the open place where the council of elders sat.

Before the elders stood a tall Karen peddler. His robes were covered with the dust of a hard journey. "Hear my report, oh noble elders of Chinwa. I bring a warning from the north. A mighty herd of wild elephants have come down from the hills to feed on the rice harvest. Many paddy fields have been flattened. Whole villages have been destroyed."

"Are the elephants coming this way?" asked an elder.

"Ay. They come down this valley," replied the Karen. "I have been sent to warn you. Majda Koom leads the wild herd. He is the cause of this. He fears nothing. Noisemakers and torches of fire do not stop him."

Wails of dismay went up from the villagers.

"Majda Koom has surely gone mad," said an elder. "He must be killed before harm comes to our village."

Killed! Haji choked back a cry. But when he thought for a moment, he felt better. There were no hunters in the village. They had no weapons that could harm Majda Koom.

"Send for the soldiers," said the Karen. "Let them hunt down this beast and shoot him."

"No!" The cry broke from Haji's lips like a sob. He rushed forward to face the elders. "Majda Koom is not mad! He is not mad!"

"Silence!" ordered the chief of the elders. "What nonsense is this? Have you a better plan for saving the village?" he asked Haji.

Haji swallowed and looked about in sudden confusion. Plan? He had not had time to think of a plan. The eyes of all were upon him, waiting, but his thoughts were only of his beloved elephant. Majda Koom was in danger. Something had to be done. He said the first thing that came into his head.

"Majda Koom is not mad," he said again. "He belongs to me. I, Haji, will capture him and turn back the herd. The village shall not be harmed. Let the safety of your rice fields and the village be on my head."

There were angry rumbles in the crowd.

"He speaks with the tongue of a jackal," growled the Karen. "Do not listen to him. What boy could stay the charge of a hundred wild elephants?"

"Enough of this foolish talk," cried an elder. "Send the boy away."

"Ay, send the boy away," said the chief elder. "The Karen speaks wisely. We shall send for the soldiers at once. Who will ride for them?"

Shoved roughly aside, Haji heard no more. He worked his way through the press of people and blindly struck out down the street with the speed of a black panther.

Where he was going he did not know—nor did he care. What difference could it make? Majda Koom would soon be shot and nothing could be done to save him, nothing at all.

8

Secret of the Little Temple Bell

He ran until he reached the river. There his friend
Ket Kay caught up with him.

"Never have I known one as brave as you, Haji,"
he gasped in admiration. "They did not believe your
words, but I believe them. Where do you go now?"

Haji brushed the hot tears from his face. Across
the river he saw the lonely cliff where the sayah—
the witch doctor—lived, and he remembered the
strange powers of magic charms. That was it. A
magic charm! It would be just the thing.

"I go to the sayah," he said recklessly.

Ket Kay gasped. He glanced at the cliff, at the
sunset sky. "At this hour?" he asked.

Pretending not to be afraid, Haji tugged at the boat

63

drawn up on the shore. Ket Kay helped him drag it into the water, for it was heavy, hollowed out of a log.

The cliff was a place of mysterious moans and groans and rattling things where few villagers cared to venture even by the light of day. Haji brushed aside his fears. There was no time to lose if Majda Koom was to be saved.

Daylight faded quickly as they paddled across the

river. Where the evening shadows were gathering under the cliff, they found the climbing path. It grew darker as they started up, and the sky above seemed to fade to the color of blood. Surely this was an evil place. The cliff, and even the sky above, seemed to have fallen under the magic spell of the powerful sayah.

Halfway up they were startled by a sound—an eerie, wailing sound that might have been the wind in the lonely rock crags. But there was no wind.

The boys looked at each other. Ket Kay's eyes were so wide they looked white. He took a step backward.

"The sayah might be angry if two of us come," he whispered. "I shall wait for you here."

Haji nodded and went on alone. He could not turn back now. Cold chills went up and down his back, and he wondered what kind of creature this was that had such powers over the evil nat spirits.

Presently, he reached the top and stood before a cave covered with tiger skins. Scattered about the entrance were broken bones and tufts of fur and feathers, as if hyenas had feasted there.

The wailing sound, which came from within the cave, suddenly stopped.

"On what business did you come?" asked a high-pitched voice.

Haji at last found his tongue. "M-make me a charm to keep wild elephants away."

"What price will you pay?"

Haji had not thought of payment. "I—I have nothing."

"Nothing!" screeched the voice behind the tiger skins.

"It is to save the village and the life of Majda Koom," pleaded Haji.

Angry rattling and hissing sounds came from the cave.

Haji trembled, afraid he might have offended the powerful sayah. "Tell me the price," he begged. "Let me serve you. I will—"

"Away!" screeched the voice. "Away with you, and be quick. Darkness comes on swift wings and the nats do not wait with their curses."

Haji fled, running down the path. To be cursed by the wicked nats would surely mean death to himself and Majda Koom. He rejoined Ket Kay at the base of the cliff.

They crossed back over the river again and returned to the village even more quickly than they had left it.

In the thickening twilight, cooking fires glowed before the houses on both sides of the street like angry red eyes. A strange restlessness hung over the village. People spoke in low, anxious voices. The soldiers had been sent for, they said. It would take them a day to come.

Here and there at the edge of the village, men were gathering torches with which to frighten the elephants.

"Why do you gather torches?" Ket Kay asked one of them. "Did you not hear the Karen say Majda Koom fears nothing?"

"Ay, we heard the Karen," replied the man. "It may be that Majda Koom fears nothing. But when he is shot by the soldiers, we will frighten the other elephants away with our torches. Without their brave leader, they can be frightened easily."

Haji turned away. He did not want to hear any more talk of Majda Koom being shot. It was too horrible to think about.

As he wandered restlessly through the village with Ket Kay, they met old ones and lame ones who were already carrying their blankets and cooking pots beyond the stone wall near the pagoda temple, where the elephants could not trample them.

"If only there was something I could do," said Haji.

"Why don't you do what you told the elders you would do?" asked Ket Kay. "Go into the jungle and call Majda Koom."

Haji shook his head. "Even if I found him he would not know me. In two years I have grown tall. My voice has changed. My smell is wrong, too. I smell of the paddy fields now. If there was only some way I could make him remember me."

Ket Kay pulled his ear and blinked as thoughtfully as a frog. "Come," he said. "Maybe there is a way. We shall ask the wise one at the pagoda temple."

It seemed like a good idea. It was dark now, and approaching the temple, they moved wide around the flat stone under which the sacred cobra had its hole.

In the flickering light of the temple, before the gilded image of the Holy One, they found the old priest who knew more, and said less, than anyone else in the rice valley. He had a round, gentle face, and long fingernails on his left hand. He listened to them with patience, nodding wisely now and then. Yet he did not offer to tell them how Majda Koom could be made to recognize Haji.

"Sit here," he told them. "Meditate. All is possible for those who have found favor."

Haji took a seat on the cool stone floor. He lifted his eyes to the golden image beyond the weaving banners of smoke that rose from the incense pots. He waited eagerly, listening for an answer from the mysterious spirits of the temple.

The great gong crashed. Its booming shook the air of the temple, then faded to a thousand humming echoes. Silence came again, and the small whisperings of night.

For long minutes the priest chanted his prayers. He clicked his prayer beads and sometimes rang the small brass bell of his ceremony. But one hour passed, and another—and no answer came.

When Haji finally left the temple it seemed to him that even the gods had forsaken him. But as he turned his steps toward home, he was not at all certain of that. Something troubled him, something about the little brass bell of the ceremony. He kept remembering the sound of it. Why? Was there some secret it wished to tell?

All at once, he stopped short. He knew! He had the answer. The little brass bell reminded him of yet another bell, the great wooden bell of Majda Koom that lay at his father's bedside. Of course, that was it!

His heart pounding with new hope, Haji raced for home. He caught up the wooden bell and ran to one of the watchtowers in the rice fields, where Ket Kay awaited him.

"Look, Ket Kay!" he shouted as he climbed the bamboo ladder to the platform high over the fields. "Here is the answer. The bell of Majda Koom! I should have thought of it before. The bell has not changed its voice. Majda Koom will remember it when I ring it for him."

Ket Kay looked at the bell Haji had brought. "Good. Now you must find Majda Koom."

"Ay," replied Haji. "At dawn I go into the jungle."
He stretched out on his back. "It will not be easy
to find him. Let me rest till the big star shines over
the bend of the river."

9

Wild Elephant Raid

For a time he dozed, trying to sleep so that he would be well rested for his long journey through the jungle.

Presently, something brought him out of his sleep. He was suddenly wide awake, and he could not understand why. He sat up.

"What is it?" Ket Kay asked.

"I don't know. Did you hear anything?"

"There was nothing to hear."

That was odd, Haji thought. He knew only that his keen senses had brought him a warning. He listened, turning his head this way and that.

Somewhere in the paddy a porcupine called softly to its mate. Frogs and crickets were singing their usual songs to the starry heavens. But Haji knew these sounds would not have awakened him.

Perhaps it was not a sound at all. He tested the cool night breeze coming down from the jungled hills, and his sensitive nostrils caught a familiar smell, like the spicy fragrance of crushed grasses.

"Elephants!" he whispered. "A big herd, and very close, too, or I couldn't smell them."

"Do you think Majda Koom—"

"Look!" Haji pointed to a dark shape moving into the paddy.

Other shapes followed. Like ghostly shadows they

76

came, large elephants and small, slipping quietly out from the fringe of the jungle to feast on the precious rice.

Ket Kay grabbed Haji's arm so hard it hurt. "All our rice will be eaten. The soldiers will not be here until tomorrow. What can we do?"

"I don't know," Haji said. He had hoped to find the elephants in the jungle, before they reached the rice fields. Even the tame animals from the elephant camp would be hard to manage if they got in a rice field.

The whole margin of the jungle now was alive with shadowy motion. On they came, without making a sound. Haji had never seen such a large herd. He bent forward, trying to locate Majda Koom.

"Quick!" Ket Kay said. "Ring the bell of Majda Koom!"

An elephant hungry for rice would pay no attention to a bell, Haji knew. But he rang the bell just the same, more to please Ket Kay than anything else.

The voice of the bell brought the boys in the other watchtowers to life. They saw the elephants and began shouting and banging gongs and throwing stones to frighten away the herd. The hail of stones and the noise merely annoyed the elephants.

Haji did not like this. If the boys made the elephants angry there would be bad trouble. Stones and noise were not going to stop a mighty herd.

But one of the stones must have found its mark, for suddenly, above the din, came a scream and a crash. A watchtower disappeared at the end of the field. There were more screams from the boys, and more crashes.

"It's Majda Koom," cried Haji. "They made him angry with their stones. Now he's charging the towers!"

In frozen horror, the boys watched.

"We'll all be killed," cried Ket Kay. "Now he's coming this way! Do something, Haji. Stop him!"

What could he do? Down went the towers, one by one. Boys leaped for their lives as the bamboo frames of the towers exploded beneath them. Haji couldn't think. He couldn't move. Was there nothing that could stop that furious charge?

Down the line of towers rushed the enraged ele-

phant. He smacked into the tower next to theirs and over it went with a sickening crash.

"Here he comes!" screamed Ket Kay.

"Jump aside when he rams," Haji told him. "Jump that way. No harm will come if you hide in the rice and leave him alone."

In his haste to get ready for the leap, Ket Kay accidentally kicked the wooden elephant bell from the platform. Not that it mattered. It could not help them now.

Haji had no thought of saving himself. The mighty beast would soon pass under the platform as he rammed their tower. He had to be stopped if the rice fields and the village were to be saved. But how?

He had only seconds to think, for rushing at them out of the night came the giant elephant, trumpeting with rage.

Only one thing could stop him now—fear! If he could be frightened somehow, his fear would spread through the entire elephant herd like wildfire. They would scatter in panic and never come back.

"I have to try to scare him," Haji thought. His heart hammered as he braced himself. There was

still hope, still a chance, if he could do it right. If he failed, he would die.

He waited till the elephant was almost beneath him. Then, with the savage snarl of a tiger breaking from his lips, he jumped.

Nimble as a cat he twisted in mid-air and came down where he wanted to land—squarely on the back of the huge elephant.

Majda Koom was taken completely by surprise. His screams of terror filled the night. He turned in sudden panic and bolted for the jungle, as if ten tigers were clawing his back.

Haji clung desperately with fingers and toes. With all the power of his lungs, he kept snarling like a royal tiger making a kill.

He could hear the frightened trumpeting of the other elephants. Panic spread through the big herd. They had seen their great leader frightened off by some mysterious attack, and now they scattered and fled from the unknown danger.

Haji saw them disappearing into the jungle far to the left of him. A tight smile came to his lips. He had won. His plan had worked. The village and rice fields were saved, and none of them would ever re-

turn, for elephants never came back to a place where
they had been badly frightened.

But Haji had little time to be pleased with himself. The wild, swaying ride took all his attention
and strength. Now he had to find a way to escape
from Majda Koom—if he could. It wouldn't be easy.

He did not think he could hang on the broad back

for long. His fingers were not strong enough to dig into the rough hide. There was nothing to which he could hold. One slip would bring sudden death, for if he fell, the desperate beast would wheel instantly and trample him into the earth in a few seconds.

When they were deep in the jungle, Majda Koom slackened his pace suddenly. Haji caught his breath. The battle for his life was just beginning.

Without warning, the great trunk lashed back at him. It whipped so close to his face he could feel the wind of it. Again and again Majda struck out with his trunk, mighty blows that could have crushed the skull of a tiger. But Haji knew how far back an elephant could reach with its trunk and stayed clear.

Then Majda abruptly changed his method of attack. Tossing his mighty head, he reared, went up and up and over on his back to crush the unknown thing beneath him, just as See Po had killed the tiger.

Haji was not to be caught so easily. He jumped aside at the last moment.

With a rumble of disgust, the big tusker rolled over on its side. As it made to rise, Haji sprang up on a huge hind knee and vaulted to the broad back again.

"Tah! Tah! Stand up! Stand up!" he shouted.
"I am not a tiger. I am Haji."

Now that they were alone in the jungle, Haji began to hope that somehow, by his actions and words, he could make Majda Koom recognize him.

"If I had not lost your bell in the rice field," he said, "you would soon remember me."

The sound of his voice seemed only to anger the beast. It went off through the brush and made for the river. Soon it was splashing out through the shallows.

"Ay, big brother," said Haji. "What you need is a bath in the river. Perhaps it will cool your temper."

The big bull made a rumbling answer in his throat and plowed deeper and deeper into the river, until at last the muddy water closed over the elephant completely. Soon the water was up to Haji's neck. Then he had to swim. All he could see of Majda, who was walking on the bottom, was the tip of the trunk, held above water for breathing.

It reminded Haji of the water game they had played so often together. He looked at the tip of the trunk only a few feet ahead of him. To play the game he had only to swim over, grab the trunk, and pull it below the surface. Did Majda Koom want him to play the game now? Was the animal testing him to find out if he really was the boy Haji?

There was no way of being sure. Haji was afraid to go near. How could he be certain the trunk would not coil about him and drag him down to an awful death?

Slowly the tip of the trunk moved toward the far shore. Once it stopped and waved from side to side, as if inviting Haji to grab it.

Then suddenly the trunk disappeared altogether. Haji knew what that meant. It was the trick of a killer elephant!

10

Majda Koom's Battle with Haji

In the muddy water an elephant could turn unseen below the surface and drag down a swimmer in
a matter of moments. Haji took no chances. He
dived, found the elephant's tail, and hung on. So
long as he could hang onto the tail and hold his breath
he was safe enough.

Twice he had to kick up to the surface for air, and
dive for the tail again. But when Majda Koom
emerged on the far bank of the river, Haji was once
again perched on his back.

Again the mighty elephant had failed to get rid
of him. But the battle was far from over. With a
bellow of rage as big as six tiger roars, Majda Koom
rammed into the thickest of the jungle to brush the
pesky man-thing from his back.

It was what Hadji had most dreaded. He would be helpless against such an attack. A terrible fear gripped him as they smashed headlong through snarled entanglements that lashed and tore at his body.

Though he flattened down, it did not help him. There was no protection against the scraping jungle. Branches clubbed him. Twigs jabbed into his flesh like hot needles. Thorns ripped the length of his back till he cried out in pain. No one could take such bruising punishment for long.

Again and again he screamed for Majda to stop.

Tears blinded him. Dizziness and pain took the strength from his body. His fingers grew numb. The end was near, he knew, for he couldn't hold on much longer. Death would come quickly and take away the pain. He was thankful for that.

Just when he thought he would have to give up, a strange thing happened. The terrible punishment ceased as quickly as it had begun. They were in the open now, rushing through milky morning mists. It was almost too good to be true.

Cautiously, Haji raised his head to look in front

of them. Too late he saw the branch—a low branch coming at him like a swinging club.

It struck with a solid jolt. Stars burst in his head. The world spun and dipped and turned on edge, so that he couldn't tell up from down. It began to grow dark. For a terrible instant he hung on, fighting the swirling grayness that was closing over him.

But it closed down just the same. He went limp. He could feel his fingers lose their hold. He was slipping . . . slipping . . . sliding off into space . . . falling down, down, down into a bottomless pit of darkness.

It seemed like a long and restless sleep. And when he opened his eyes at last, the sun was lacing down through leafy bowers in the roof of the Burma jungle. How peaceful it was! Flies buzzed around him. Birds were chattering.

Nothing seemed quite real at first. It felt good to rest. But after a time, he remembered his fall from the elephant's back. His arms and legs felt as stiff as sticks, and his head hurt where the branch had struck him.

Slowly, he tested his arms, then his legs. He could move them. He felt of his head. There was a lump on the top. That was all. There was nothing to worry about. He could get up and go home as soon as he had rested.

For a time, he tried to sleep. Then, suddenly, all the little lazy sounds of the jungle morning were shattered by the loud flopping of elephant ears.

Haji sat up with a start. His eyes went wide.

Only a few feet away stood the mighty Majda Koom, swaying gently back and forth, as elephants usually do. Majda stopped swaying. They looked at each other.

For an endless moment, Haji forgot to breathe. He had not been trampled—not yet—but he knew that was not the miracle it seemed. When he had fallen and hit the ground, he had lain there in a lifeless heap—and elephants rarely attacked anything that did not move or show some sign of life.

But now! Now that he had moved, what would the elephant do? Had it waited to kill him? Or had it touched and smelled of his body and recognized him?

As if in answer, Majda reached slowly out with his long trunk. He touched Haji's chest gently as he had done so many times before, and made the small whistling sounds of a happy elephant.

A cry broke from Haji's lips. With both hands he caught the trunk and laid his cheek against it. Majda Koom knew him and loved him still!

Two years, two long years of waiting and hoping —and now it was over. They were back together again. Haji knew his father had been right. An elephant's eyes were not very sharp at a distance. All Majda had needed was a close look at him, and to touch and smell of him.

Late the following afternoon, with Haji riding proudly on the mighty head of his tusker, they entered the elephant camp. In a moment, the entire camp was in an uproar. People came running from all directions, and among them were Ket Kay and several others from the village.

"I said you would bring him here!" cried Ket Kay. "They did not believe me, but I knew it. We told how you saved the village. They did not want to believe that either."

Byoo, Haji's young friend from the elephant camp, stared. "We believe it now," he said. "It is Majda Koom. No one but Haji could have brought him back."

The villagers from Chinwa pressed through the crowd and one of them said, "The elders have sent us to take you back to the village for a day. They wish to honor you."

Oo Yan, the chief of the oozies, was nodding his head. "It is well," he said. "For one day he may go. But you will remind your elders that this boy is one of the elephant people. He belongs here with us."

At a word from Haji, the great tusker lowered him

to the ground with his trunk. Haji turned to face Thakin Jensen and the amazed oozies. Thakin Jensen still acted as if he could hardly believe what he saw.

Oo Yan stepped forward and placed a hand warmly on Haji's shoulder. "If our faith in you has been small, my son, you have at last opened our eyes. You have done what our best oozies could not do."

Ket Kay's dark eyes sparkled. "I knew he would do it. I knew it! Was there ever anyone so brave?"

Slowly a smile grew on Thakin Jensen's lips. "Many are brave," he said. "What this boy Haji has done

took far more than courage. It took love—the kind of love that a great oozie has for his elephant."

Thakin Jensen turned to Oo Yan. "Majda Koom will need careful watching for a time. See that no one handles him but this boy, and make sure the boy is properly trained as an oozie."

The oozies smiled and nodded. The wrinkled one said, "Truly this boy is the son of his father. He will make a good oozie."

Oo Yan seemed more pleased than anyone. He raised his hands for silence. "Hail! Hail to the new oozie of Majda Koom!"

Loudly and long, they hailed him.

Haji could not keep the painful lump from swelling in his throat, or the tears from his eyes. He stepped back and, resting one of his hands on a great curved tusk of his elephant, stood proudly.

Then a smile broke upon his lips, for he heard the best hail of all. It came from the great beast beside him—the happy whistling sounds of the lord of all elephants.